DISCARD

P9-DDI-186

GRUMP GROAN GROWL

By bell hooks
Illustrated by Chris Raschka

DISNEY HYPERION
Los Angeles   New York

Text copyright © 2008 by bell hooks
Illustrations copyright © 2008 by Chris Raschka
All rights reserved. Published by Disney • Hyperion, an imprint of Disney Book Group.
No part of this book may be reproduced or transmitted in any form or by any means,
electronic or mechanical, including photocopying, recording, or by any information storage
and retrieval system, without written permission from the publisher. For information address
Disney • Hyperion, 125 West End Avenue, New York, New York 10023.
First Hardcover Edition, April 2008
First Paper-Over-Board Edition, November 2017
10 9 8 7 6 5 4 3 2 1
FAC-029191-17272
Printed in Malaysia
Library of Congress Cataloging-in-Publication Control Number for Hardcover Edition:
2007022312
ISBN 978-1-368-00782-5
Reinforced binding
Visit www.DisneyBooks.com

RO451727706

for MARCUS
best boy—
beloved reader
–bh

For bell
–CR

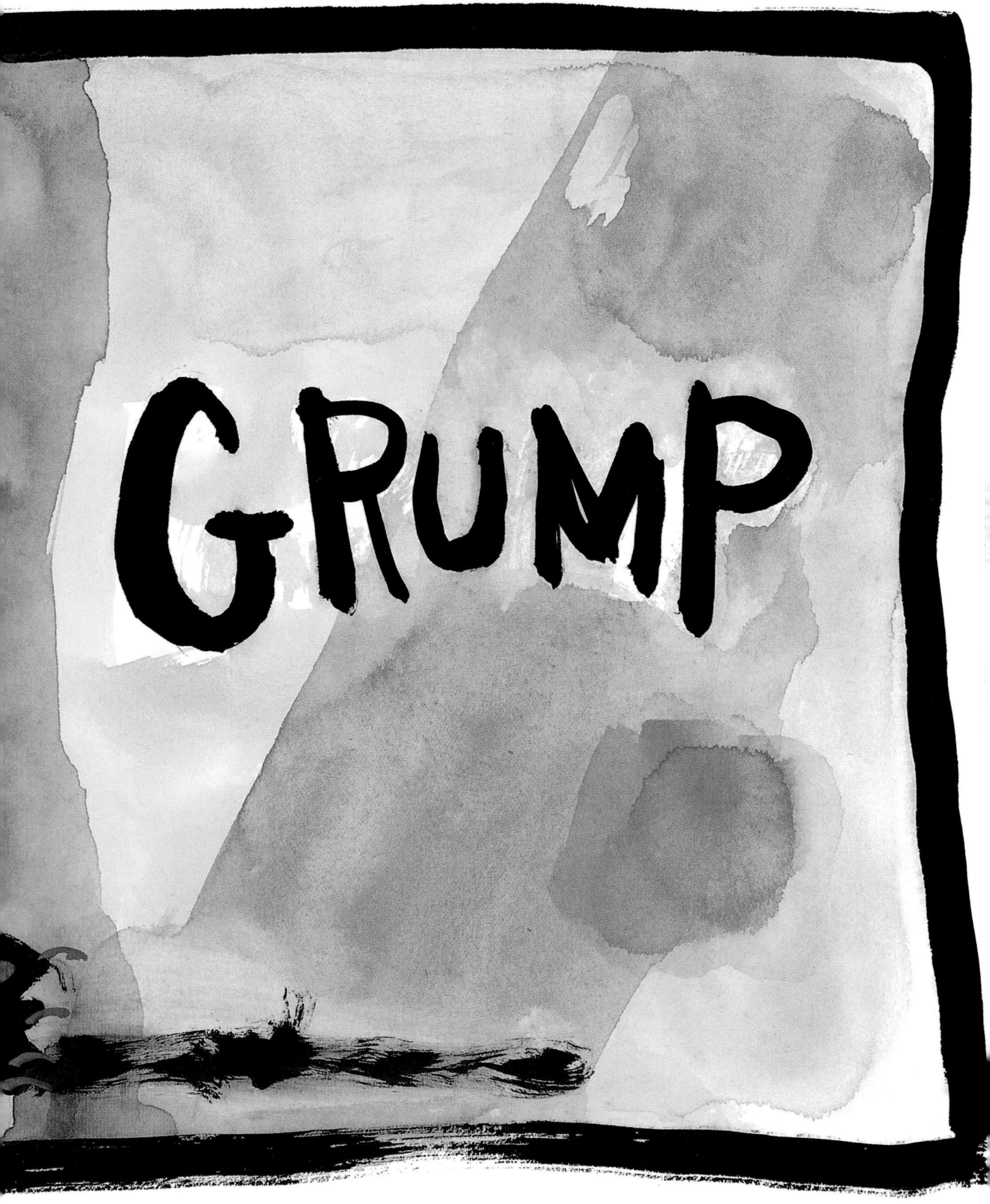
GRUMP

GROAN

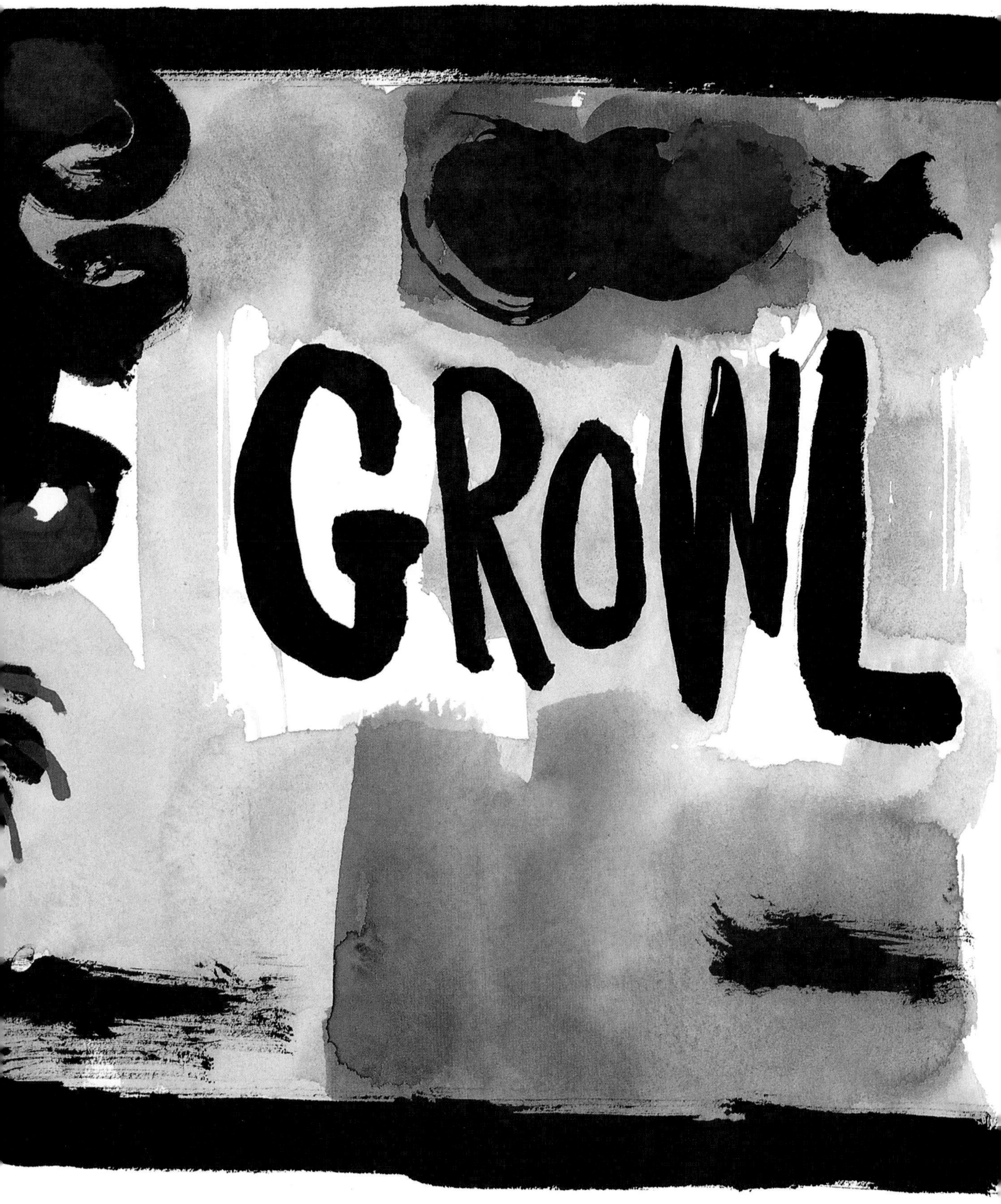
GROWL

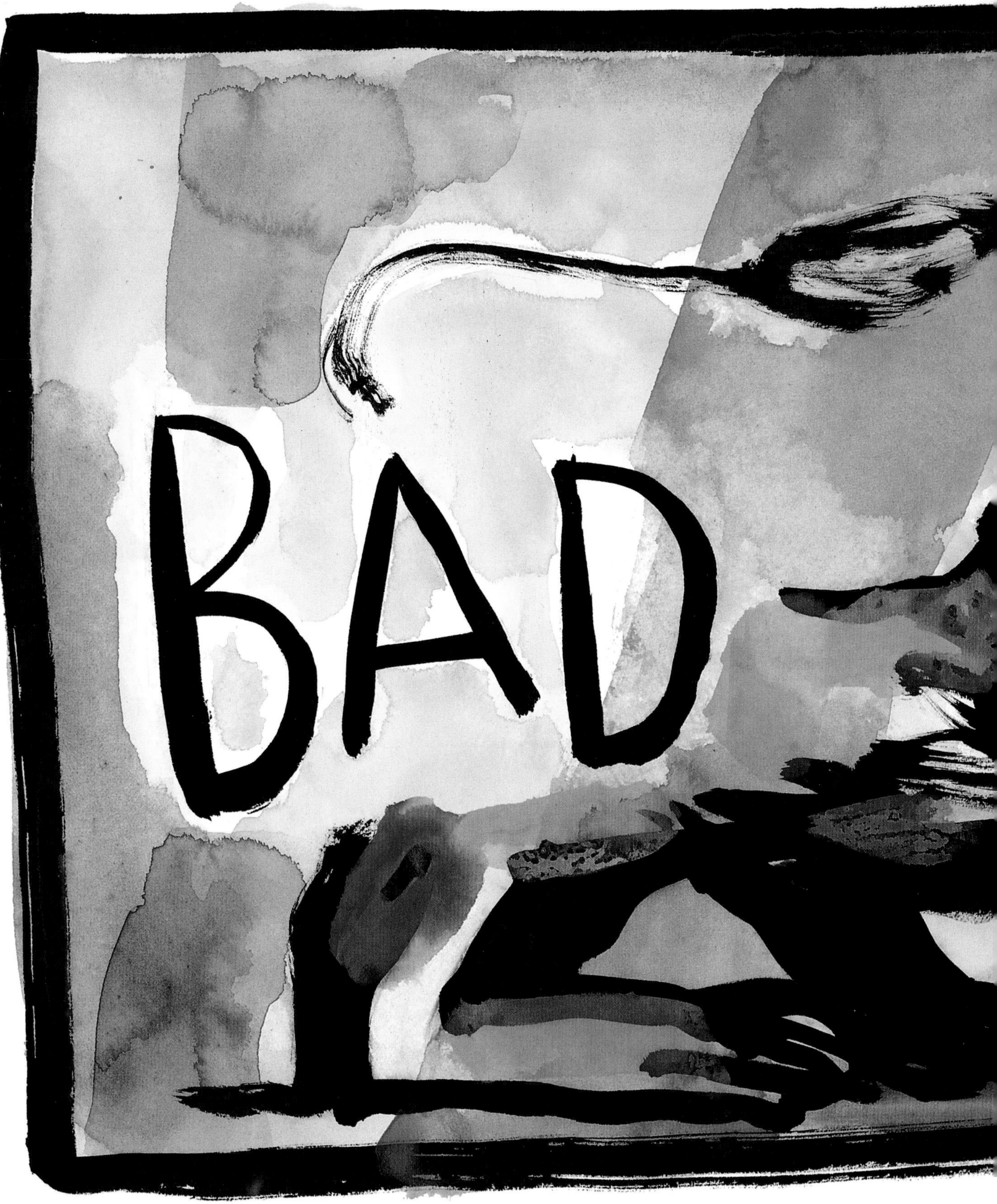
BAD

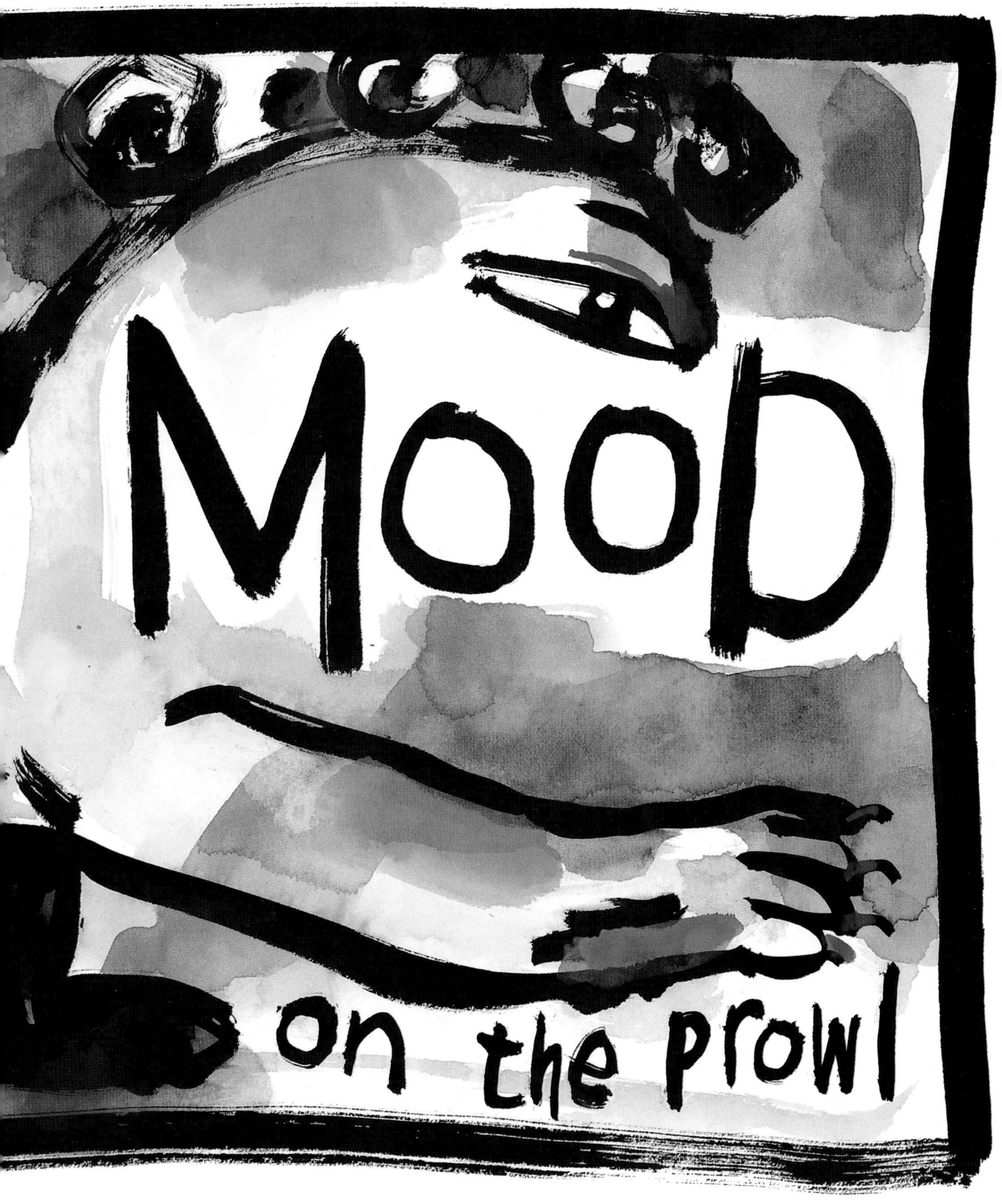
MOOD
on the prowl

CAN'T STAND OUTSIDE

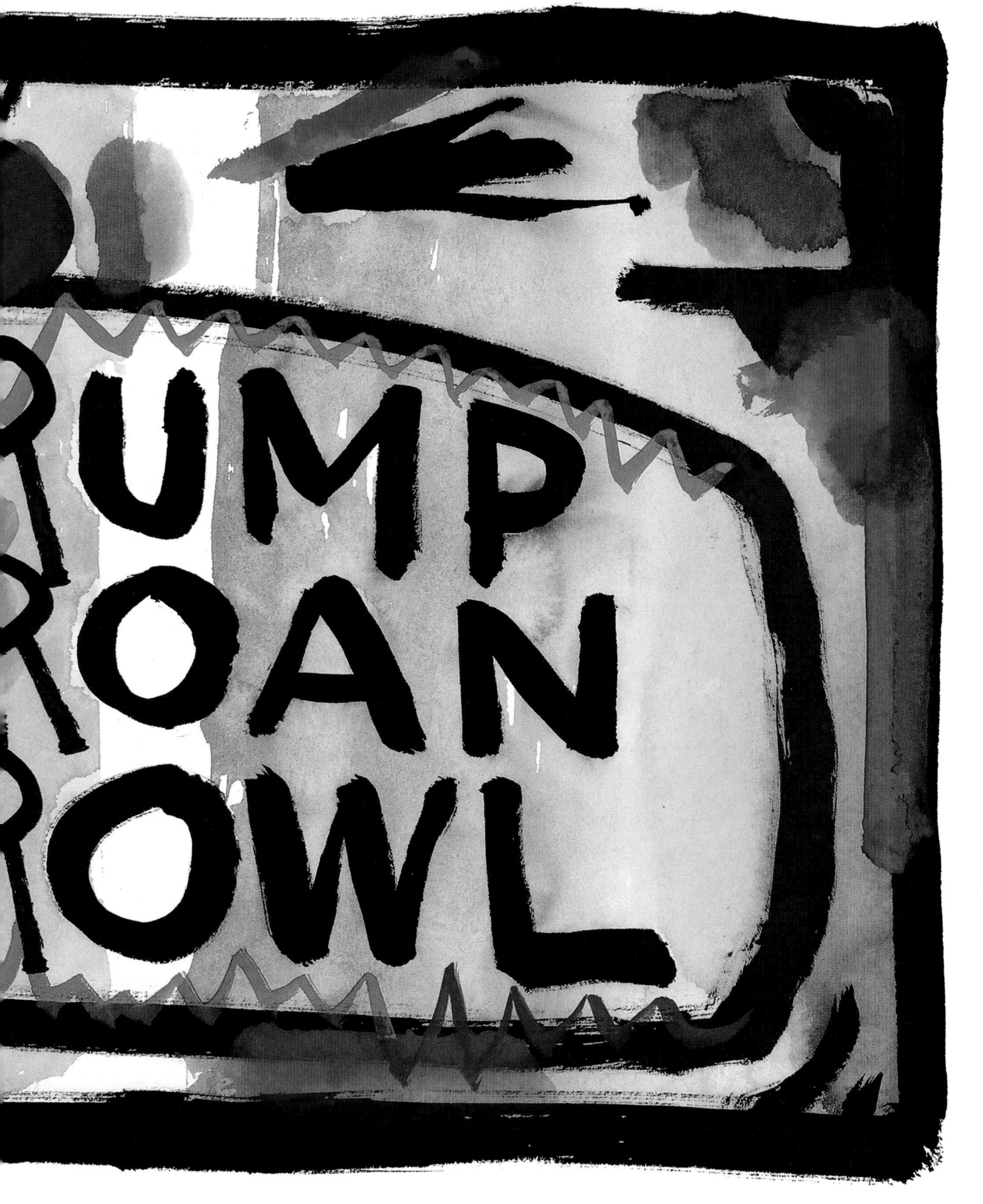
RUMP
ROAN
OWL

ALL I AM IS

BAD MOOD
on the PROWL

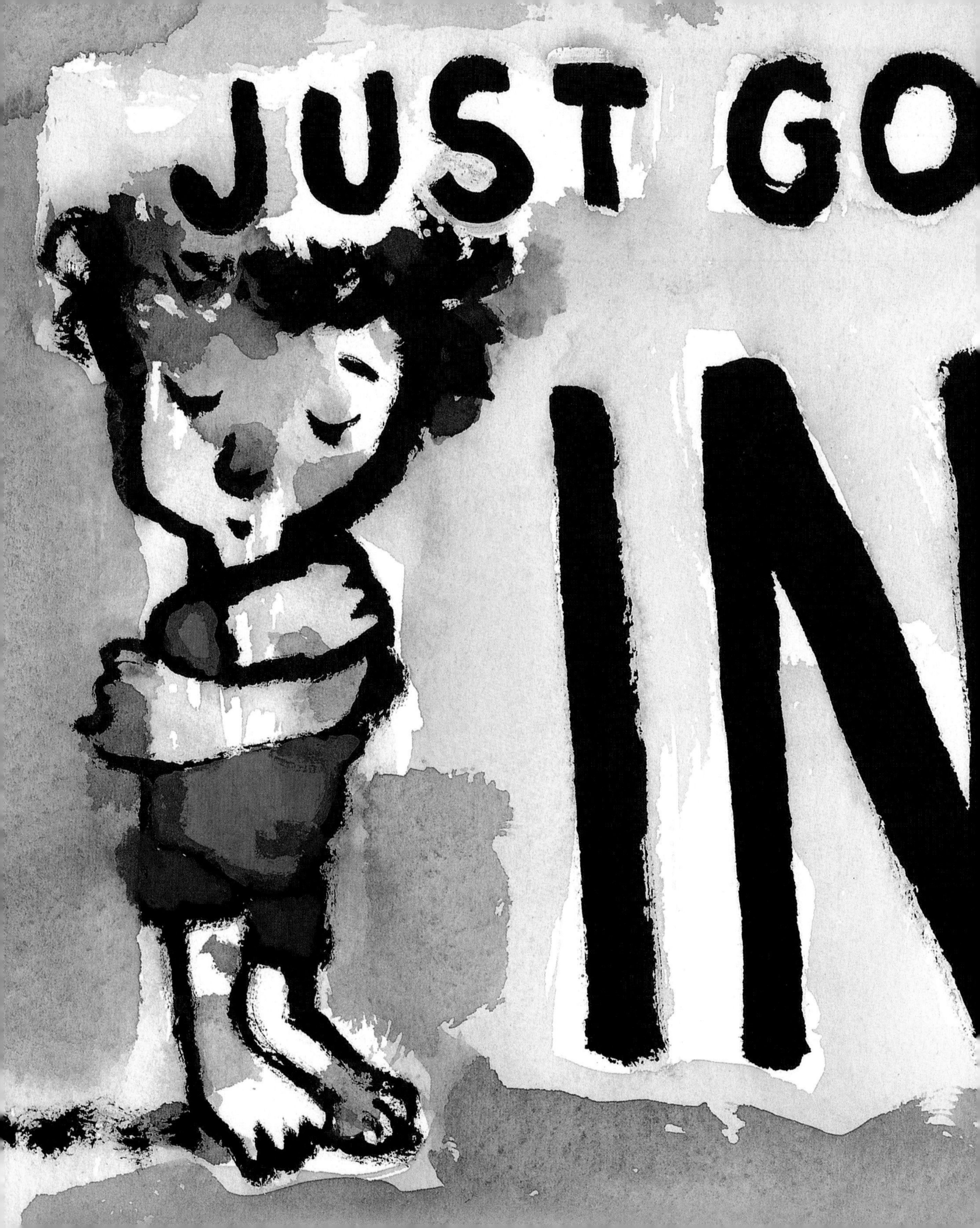
JUST GO
IN

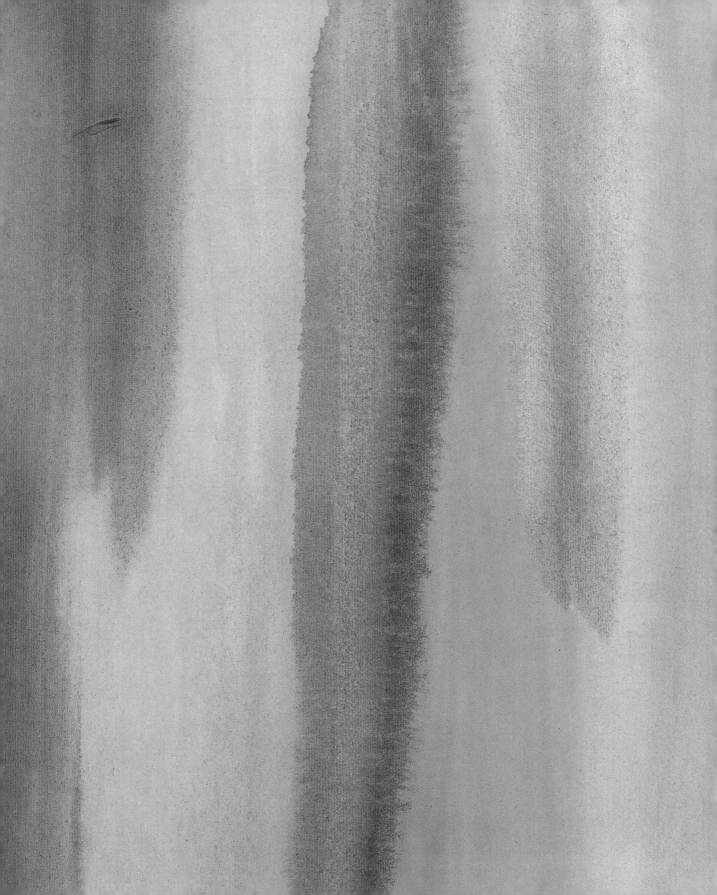